THIS CANDLEWICK BOOK BELONGS TO:

_____

_____

_____

To my love, Saeed,
who played soccer in the street every day
M. J.

To my mentor, C. F. Payne
A. G. F.

Text copyright © 2010 by Mina Javaherbin
Illustrations copyright © 2010 by A. G. Ford

First paperback edition 2012

The Library of Congress has cataloged the hardcover edition as follows:

Javaherbin, Mina.
Goal! / Mina Javaherbin ; illustrated by A. G. Ford. — 1st ed.
p. cm.
Summary: In a dangerous alley in a township in South Africa, the strength and unity which a group of
young friends feel while playing soccer keep them safe when a gang of bullies arrives to cause trouble.
ISBN 978-0-7636-4571-7 (hardcover)
[1. Soccer—Fiction. 2. Bullies—Fiction. 3. Friendship—Fiction.
4. South Africa—Fiction.] I. Ford, A. G., ill. II. Title.
PZ7.J327Goc 2010
[E]—dc22   2008047266

ISBN 978-0-7636-5822-9 (paperback)

18 19 20 21 CCP 10 9 8

Printed in Shenzhen, Guangdong, China

This book was typeset in Archetype.
The illustrations were done in oil.

Candlewick Press
99 Dover Street
Somerville, Massachusetts 02144

visit us at www.candlewick.com

GOAL!

Mina Javaherbin

illustrated by A. G. Ford

CANDLEWICK PRESS

I HAVE TO GET water from the well before dark.
But I finished my homework, and right now it's soccer time.

"Jamal, Hassan, Magubani, Keto, Badu!"
I call for my friends.
No one runs out to play.
The streets are not always safe.

Left is clear.
Right is clear.

I reach into one bucket and lift out
my prize for being the best reader in class.
I am the proud owner of a
new federation-size football.

Keto comes out of his house.

I kick the ball to him.

"Ajani!" he calls.

"No more old plastic balls!" Jamal says.

He kicks his old ball to the side,

sending a flip-flop into the air.

Magubani, Hassan, and Badu come out.

We pass the shiny leather ball in a circle.

We are real champions, playing with a real ball.

With my buckets, I set up the goal.

Left is clear.
Right is clear.

The streets are not safe,
but I have a plan:
"We'll take turns guarding for bullies."
I pick Keto and Jamal for my team.
Hassan picks Magubani and Badu.
We draw sticks. Badu gets the shortest one.
He is the first to stand guard on the roof.

I kick off to Jamal.
Magubani, fast,
steals the ball.
Keto steals it back,
fakes a kick to the left.

When we play,
we forget to worry.
When we run,
we are not afraid.

Keto shoots to the right.
"Corner kick!" Jamal and I cheer.
When we play,
we feel strong.
Hassan and Magubani complain, "No fair.
Our teammate's on the roof."
I secretly point to Jamal's flip-flops
and whisper to them,
"Two against two. Fair."

We kick.
We dribble.
We run
after our brilliant ball.

I follow the ball to the end of the alley;
I follow the ball to the end of the world;
I follow the black and white patches
like a Bafana Bafana footballer.

"Corner, corner!" Keto, Jamal, and I shout.
"It's not a corner," Badu calls from the rooftop.
  We disagree.
  I shoot for the goal
  and knock a bucket down.
"Goal!" Keto cheers.
  Badu jumps down and shouts,
"No way. No goal when the bucket falls."

And suddenly we see them.

We are trapped.

Quickly, I stand in front of the ball —
give it a swift reverse kick into the bucket.
Hassan tilts the bucket back down,
hiding the ball.

"What do we have here?" the tall boy asks.

"We're just playing football," I say.

"Just football?" he says, and walks to me.

I do not breathe and nod yes.

"Is this your ball?"

He pushes me aside and sets our old ball on top of the bucket.

"Say good-bye to your ball then," he says, and laughs.

I panic. If he kicks the ball, the bucket will tip
over and . . .

Jamal covers his face with his hands.
The tall guy snatches the ball.
The bucket wobbles.
My heart sinks.
In slow motion, the bucket stops.

The tall guy fastens the plastic ball onto his bicycle.

Jamal pretends to cry.

We follow his lead.

"Crybabies," the tall boy says.

"No playing soccer here or you'll be sorry."

"Chickens!" says another.

They laugh at us,

get on their rickety bikes, and leave.

We wait for them to get far away.

Jamal climbs to the rooftop.
"Do-over!" he calls,
holding our federation-size ball
over his head
like it's the World Cup that we've all won.

Right is clear.
Left is clear.

Badu wants to guard again.

He promises not to jump down this time.

I kick off to Keto.

Magubani steals the ball.

Keto steals it back, shoots.

Hassan blocks with his chest,

bumps the ball in the air.

I get in

with a head to Keto.

Keto shoots to Jamal.

Magubani has the ball.
He passes to Hassan.
Hassan runs.
I steal from Hassan
and *whoosh* like the wind,
glued to the ball.
I dribble past him and—

Goooooooal!

Left is clear.
Right is clear.

Down the alley, as far as we can see is clear.
The streets are not safe here.
But we have a plan.
When we play,
the sound
of our kicks
on the ball
is music.

When we play together,
we are unbeatable.

AUTHOR'S NOTE

The game of soccer—called *football* in most nations outside the United States and Canada—has been around for thousands of years. During the Middle Ages, kings and rulers banned soccer because they wanted men to go to war instead of gathering together to play. The punishment for playing soccer was death!

To this day, in the face of poverty, bully rulers, and unsafe alleys, people play soccer. Through war, revolution, and hardship, people play soccer. In South Africa, East Asia, North America, the West Indies, and in all corners of the world, people play soccer. Soccer bonds. Soccer makes both young and old feel that they belong, that they matter, and that they can win.

In South Africa, the people affectionately call their national football team *Bafana Bafana,* "the boys." Here in this alley, we join a group of friends as they embrace the spirit of soccer. They play to stay connected. They play to stay children. They play to stay human. But mostly, they play to play.

Mina Javaherbin told stories before she knew how to write them down. Born in Iran, she immigrated to the United States and is a practicing architect. She likes to look for what we share around the world and believes that the most personal experiences are the most universal ones. Sometimes she calls herself a world citizen. About *Goal!*, she says, "Football is magic to me. Where there is a ball, there's hope, laughter, and strength." Mina Javaherbin currently lives in southern California. This is her debut picture book.

A. G. Ford is the illustrator of *Barack* by Jonah Winter, a *New York Times* bestseller, and *Michelle* by Deborah Hopkinson. He also contributed to *Our Children Can Soar: A Celebration of Rosa, Barack, and the Pioneers of Change* by Michelle Cook. About *Goal!*, he says, "Rich skin tones, textured shanty homes, and luminous skies—a delightful story to illustrate." A. G. Ford lives in Texas.